Avocado Varieties

Reed

Maluma

Fuerte

Lula

Hass

Pinkerton

Gwen

Brogden

Bacon

Long Neck

Trinitario

Criollo

Forastero

The Three
Main Types
of Cacao

Printed in the United States of America
ISBN: (p) 978-1-64250-742-3
(e) 978-1-64250-743-0
www.mangopublishinggroup.com
www.flavcity.com

The Tasty Adventures

of Rose Honey

CHOCOLATE AVOCADO PUDDING

by Bobby & Dessi Parrish
Cowritten and Illustrated
by Kaloyan Nachev & Boril Nachev

Rose Honey woke up snuggled like a ball between Mommy and Daddy.
As the sun peeked through the window, Rose had a delicious idea.
Today would be the perfect day to make pudding.
But not just any ordinary pudding.
She wanted chocolate avocado pudding!
"To the Chef's Tower!" she declared.

Scooped Avocado

First, Daddy cut the avocado in half.
Inside was a large round seed.
"We can grow an avocado tree from this seed," Daddy told Rose.
Rose liked that idea and kept it to plant later.

Fresh Vanilla Beans

Vanilla Flower

Vanilla Leaves

Rose loved the sweet and floral scent of vanilla. "All we need is just a teaspoon of vanilla extract," Mommy said. "It has a very strong flavor."

Now for the chocolate part: Dad brought out the cacao powder.
Rose wanted to taste every single ingredient.
"Oooh," she said and scrunched her face.
That didn't taste anything like Mommy's chocolate brownies.
The cacao powder was bitter!

CACAO
LEAVES

CACAO
TREE

CACAO
PODS

Maple
Leaves

Maple
Tree

MAPLE
TREE
TRUNK

Maple
Tree
Sap

"How about some maple syrup
to sweeten things up!?"
Daddy asked.

Great idea! Rose loved that
sweet, sticky, brown nectar,
especially on pancakes
and waffles!

Sea Salt

"What should we add to bring out the chocolate flavor?" asked Daddy.
"Salt, Daddy, of course!" said Rose Honey.
"Two pinches with my fingers, or one with yours."

"Did you know that chocolate and orange are best friends?" asked Daddy while zesting the orange.

Orange Zest

Orange
Flower

Orange
Juice

The bright, fresh orange scent
tickled Rose's nose and she couldn't help but take a sip.
"Remember to save some for the pudding!" said Daddy.

"Mint goes great with chocolate, right?
Let's add some mint herbal tea." Rose decided.
She was ready to have a proper tea party.

MINT

CHAMOMILE

GINGER

BASIL

LINDEN

LEMON
BALM

JASMINE

MINT
TEA

SAGE

THYME

LEMON
BALM

Watch out for the scary blender!
Rose took cover as they turned the blender on.
So many colors mixed in a magical whirlwind.
Green avocado, brown cacao, black vanilla,
dark golden maple syrup, orange juice,
amber tea.

Rose looked in the blender and saw the smoothest pudding in the world. She was so excited to see this sweet treat! Light, airy, and silky smooth! Almost like Mommy's cheek.

Daddy scooped the pudding into little bowls, first for Mommy, then for him, then who else? "Me!" said Rose.

"Mmmm!" she could taste the chocolate, maple syrup,
and orange in this delicious concoction.
"Cheers, Mom and Dad!" said Rose and sipped on some mint tea.

That night, Rose dreamed of the avocado
and the big plans she had for it the next day.

The next morning, Rose put toothpicks in the avocado seed and balanced
it in a cup of water. After a few weeks, the avocado seed sprouted.

And Daddy and Mommy helped Rose plant it so it would grow into a big tree.

Baked Avocado with Shrimp and lime

Baked Avocado with Salmon and Eggs

Avocado Salad Bowl

Classic Avocado Toast

Avocado Cheesecake

Almond Avocado Fudge

Rose knew she would grow up one day too, but until then she promised herself to cook many more delicious recipes.

Mediterranean Avocado Toast

Avocado Chocolate Bars

Spicy Guacamole

Ricotta Avocado Toast

Avocado Smoothie

Avocado Ice Cream

Chocolate Avocado Pudding

INGREDIENTS:

2 ripe avocados, pitted
1 teaspoon (5 ml) vanilla extract
½ cup (35 g) unsweetened cacao powder
½ cup plus 2 tablespoons (90ml) of maple syrup
¼ teaspoon salt
zest of one orange
¼ cup (60 ml) fresh orange juice
¼ cup (60 ml) mint (or herbal) tea

PREP TIME: 5 MINUTES
COOKING TIME: 3 MINUTES
MAKES: 3 SERVINGS

Watch Rose Honey make
this delicious chocolate
avocado pudding!

DIRECTIONS:

Add everything to a blender or food processor and mix
on high until smooth and creamy. The pudding will keep
in the fridge for 2 days.

The Tasty Adventures
of Rose Honey

CINNAMON APPLE CAKE

by Bobby & Dessi Parrish
Cowritten and Illustrated
by Kaloyan Nachev & Boril Nachev

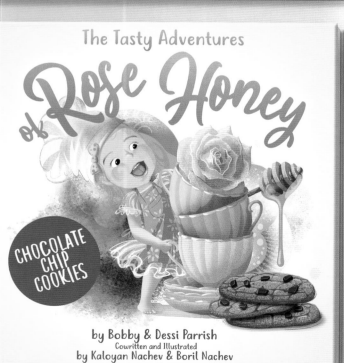

The Tasty Adventures
of Rose Honey

CHOCOLATE CHIP COOKIES

by Bobby & Dessi Parrish
Cowritten and Illustrated
by Kaloyan Nachev & Boril Nachev

JOIN THE TASTY ADVENTURES OF ROSE HONEY IN OTHER BOOKS AS WELL

CINNAMON APPLE CAKE

Rose finds herself in the land of flavors and aromas. On her journey, she learns many things and preparing a delicious cake is one of them.

CHOCOLATE CHIP COOKIES

Rose Honey loves cooking and baking with Mommy and Daddy. Chocolate chip cookies are one of her favorite treats and making them is an adventure for little Rose. Join her on this magical culinary journey.

ABOUT THE AUTHORS

Bobby and Dessi are bestselling cookbook authors with millions of followers across the world. With his popular FlavCity videos, Bobby shares grocery shopping and healthy food tips. Bobby's favorite place is in the kitchen, making delicious meals for his family.

Dessi dedicates her time to raising their daughter, Rose Honey. She also enjoys paleo baking, doing food photography, and painting.

Rose loves being involved in everything Mom and Dad do, especially in the kitchen where she helps make all kinds of tasty dishes. You can find all of Rose Honey's cooking videos on the FlavCity Facebook page. www.facebook.com/flavcity

ABOUT THE ILLUSTRATORS

Kaloyan Nachev, the illustrator and cowriter of this book, is also Dessi's brother. He is an acclaimed artist, producer, director, and screenwriter. He lives in Bulgaria where Dessi is originally from. Kaloyan has four children and loves spending time with his family. His oldest son, Boril Nachev, helped cowrite and illustrate this book. Kaloyan adores his niece Rose Honey and has a special connection with her, as she was born just a few days after his youngest daughter Petra.

Avocado Varieties

Reed

Maluma

Fuerte

Lula

Hass

Pinkerton

Gwen

Brogden

Bacon

Long Neck

Forastero

Trinitario

Criollo

The Three
Main Types
of Cacao